# the quiet calendar

## oquirrh keyes

*the quiet calendar* is a work of poetry.
Names, characters, and events are used poetically; any resemblance to actual persons, living or dead, is coincidental or used with artistic intent.

For permissions or inquiries, contact:
**Epiphany Blaire Press.**

**ISBN: 979-8-218-83859-1**
**Third Edition Revised: April 2026**
**Printed in the United States of America**

Cover design, interior layout and original artwork by Oquirrh Keyes.  All rights reserved.

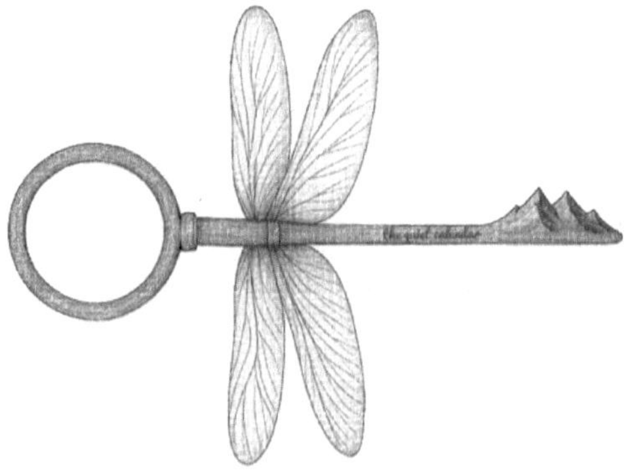

**dedication**

for my husband—whose patience and love steadied me through every silence.

for my mother—whose wisdom and gentle presence reminded me to keep going.

for my daughter, margo—whose laughter and light gave me hope when i needed it most.

and for my cousin, homeboy—whose loyalty and understanding made every day a little easier.

thank you for holding space for my healing, without judgment, and for believing in me when i could not.

6

## author's note

when grief kept time, i kept count.

this book began as a way to measure silence—
each day a note in the long song of letting go.

what started as survival became ritual; what began
as loss became clarity.

i wrote these poems in lowercase because healing
felt quiet, and lowercase made space for the quiet
to speak.

the quiet calendar is not about him.

it's about the moment i stopped needing his
silence to understand my own.

*these poems were written in real time, day by day, as the silence spoke.*

—oquirrh keyes

**table of contents**

## time not marked on the calendar



## epilogue

## about the author

grief kept time.

these pages mark the days i counted in silence.

the ache. the clarity. the return.

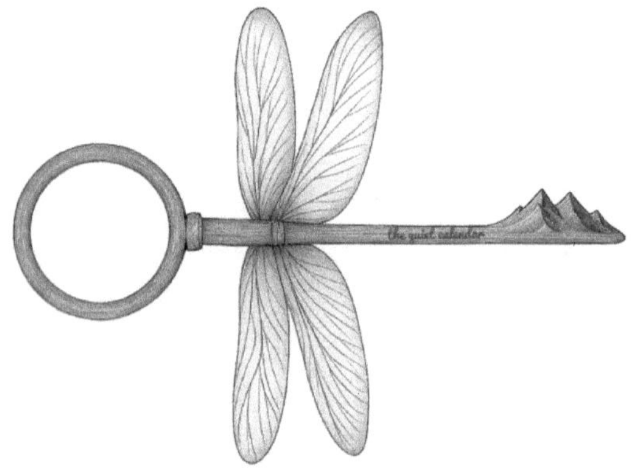
the quiet calendar

the counting

no us

# <u>day one</u>
**no us**

*i can't believe you're gone—*
*end of story. done.*

*i let my walls fall,*
*now i walk unarmed,*
*a zombie stumbling through life.*

every corner of my heart
remembers your name—
coffee,
the heat of your hand,
your beard against my cheek.

**no us.**

i sit hollow—
a body waiting,
a voice that won't come.

i don't eat.
i don't sleep.

please come back—

don't forget me.

you rigged my circuits to your rhythm.
now the lights are out.

**no us.**

you don't call.
you don't text.

**your silence—deafening.**

you're home,
smiling at your wife—
pretending i don't exist.

that thought
breaks me—
how easily
you pushed me away.

**no us.**

i grieve quietly—

lie when they ask if i'm okay—

a smile plastered on,

head nodding,

inside i'm dying.


we were supposed to be—

fate, destiny—

a love immortalized in a book.

instead, we are an

obituary. rip.


**no us.**


packing things to put away,

i found my antique playboy key—

the one that matches yours.


we found mine in an antique store,

that day we spent

pretending—

we were more.

**no us.**


tears fall,
memories—
overwhelming.

begging feels ridiculous—
and true.

would it change reality?
would my voice
call you back?

come back,

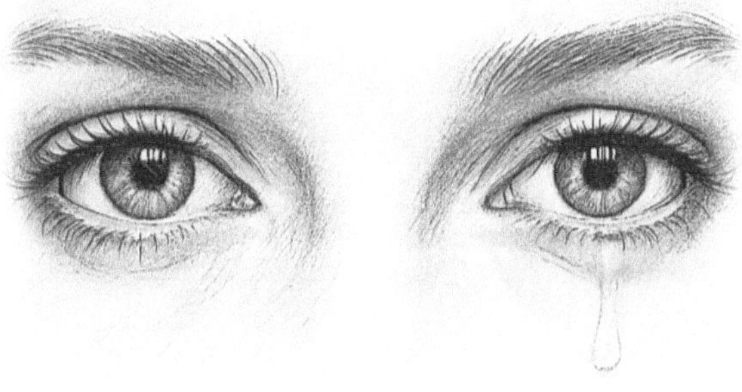

please.

**no us.**

reality keeps its distance.
memory keeps its weight.

there is no answer
that brings you back—

only the slow work
of returning to me.

so i practice small things:
a glass of water,
a breath,
a step.

**no us.**

only me,
building walls,
wearing armor,
more aware.

**<u>day two</u>**
**smoke and mirrors**

last night the fog lifted.

leaning into the glass,
i finally saw me.

ten years of smoke—
the mirror only ever showed you.

you whispered,
*"ti amo,*
*soulmates,*
*kismet,*
*fate."*

i drank the words—

tried to believe they were partly true—

just poison disguised as care,
numbing my brain
from your pain.

the smoke is gone.
i see your chess board.

the one we played on—
me, your pawn,
not special,
not loved—
just a move
to secure your ego.

checkmate.

those years full of insecurity,
questions building
inside me.

the mirror holds my face,
not yours.

the chess board is empty.
you're alone,
no pawn to control,
now the years before me,
i enter—
confidently.

i see me.

<u>**day three**</u>
**the end**

i've erased memories from my home.
realization sets in deep.


**the end**


we seemed so real.
i loved you—
still do.


hoping parts of us meant something—
that thoughts of me will linger—


maybe—
you will know regret.


**the end**


i'm inching forward,
still looking back,
hoping for your text—
my pace not lessening,
just slow.

now you, us,
only a chapter—
a painful one.

**no more**

hate is starting to
replace the good—

memories bitter—
not sweet.

i see clearer now—
a man who deceived,
took more than he ever gave
me.

**the end**

not anymore.

i won't waste my time,
my energy,
my worth,

on a man who deceived two women—
maybe more.


i said goodbye—
you tried to keep your foot in the door:
a *"ti amo,"*
an *"i'll always be here."*


this time,
i slammed the door,
locked it,
bolted it shut.


**the end.**


**no more.**

## <u>day four</u>
**seen**

going through texts and memories,

a moment of weakness—

wanting to believe

something was true.


so much confirmation avoided—

deflected questions,

silence used as a shield.


rewarding me with sweet texts—

like that was a prize.


all bullshit and lies,

delivered with kisses—

hard to detect,

when my brain was turned on

by your pheromone.


you kept me close

because i could see—

under your mask.

you—
exposed,
vulnerable.

that startled you.

my questions, my truth
threatened your perfectly crafted
deception.

not love.

fear.

fear was exciting.
it kept you guessing—
intrigued, on edge.

you liked the challenge of me,
so you kept me near—
a relationship built on my hope,
your rope.

you made me question myself,
doubt my intuition,

feel not enough.

i see you now—
a sad, lonely man
who played games,
wore masks
and called it love.

convincing himself—
he was worthy of me.

hindsight makes things clear—
in the moment,
i thought you were worthy.
i thought i was lucky,
*"tee hee."*

your lies catching up,
women dropping out of sight.

your number is up—
women unite—
word has spread:
red flag, run.
you stand alone,

clutching your phone.

and me?

i rediscovered the things i'd tossed aside:
family,
friends,
hobbies,
work.

my calendar full,
self-worth—
intact.

i am loved.

i will blossom.

my roots needed,
 water—
after the drought.

they are unbreakable now.

**<u>day five</u>**
**coffee**

it's been a month

since our spot held me.


the first weeks,

i sat there in silence,

music in my ears, still a few tears

wishing for you to appear.


you never did—

only excuses,

fear of being followed,

promises that we were ok.


i believed you.

swallowed my hurt,

called it temporary,

not goodbye.


weeks three and four,

i only drove by.

sometimes i circled back,

waiting on a text—

your words cool,

your tone distant,

still all about you.


tears came,

hope began to fade.


i started learning

the language of your lies.


by weeks five and six,

i chose something new.


coffee with me,

the morning breeze—

no waiting,

no tears.


ten years of lies,

not a promise kept—

i don't want your words,

don't send replies.

now i find comfort—

within me.


peace sits,

where pain—

once lived.


coffee mornings belong to me—

a new place,

a new meaning—

poetry.

this is about me.

<u>**day six**</u>
**24 hours**

it's been twenty-four hours
since your words lit up my phone.

i didn't reply.
i didn't even want to.

no racing pulse,
no waiting breath,
just calm—
a silence that feels like mine.

i used to ache in the quiet,
counting seconds,
pleading for you to come.

now the silence is my strength,
a place you can't access.

my walls are strong.

careless whispers
@ Oquirrh Keyes 2025
dose of reality

<u>**day seven**</u>
**one week complete**

i awoke with no thoughts of you,
no hand reaching for my phone,
no waiting for the ping of a man
i no longer know.


morning routines moved quietly,
unbothered by silence.


songs on the stereo
no longer stung—
i sang out loud and
giggled some.


later, at home with a movie,
something opened inside me.


tears came—
not grief,
release—
a waterfall welcomed,
a reminder of the good—
and still, no pain.

only understanding.


endings will always ache,
but when held with grace
they offer lessons.


memories soften,
becoming smiles instead of scars.


our chapter is over,
and i can look back
with a smile.

<u>**day eight**</u>
**lighter**

the morning felt lighter,
as if the air had shifted.

i moved through the day
without carrying you on my shoulders,
without the weight of what-ifs.

there was no need for answers,
no craving for your voice—
just a steady rhythm in my chest,
and the quiet knowledge
that i am moving on.

**<u>day nine</u>**
**squirrel**


i saw a squirrel today,
running across the lot.


all this time here,
and never once
have i seen one before.


weeks ago,
this sight would have undone me.


we spent years on squirrels—
your morning walks,
the pictures you sent,
our small thread of chatter
woven into bigger things.


back then
i would have broken.


today,
i only watched it run.

i thought of you briefly,

then let it go.


i saw a squirrel today,

and i was okay.

<u>**day ten**</u>
**no urge**

tonight i felt no urge
to reach for you.

the habit of checking,
the ache of wondering,
is loosening its grip.

i carried myself home
without looking back,
without inventing reasons
to hold on—
without fear of moving on.

the silence is lighter now,
almost like freedom—
stretching out before me.

<u>**day eleven**</u>
**untethered**

today i see the truth,

not in his words—

but in the silence between them.


he gave me fragments—

stories spun to bind me,

never the whole.


i no longer chase answers.

the pattern;

it speaks for itself.


no more lies,

no more secrecy,

no more control.


my silence is my strength—

my freedom,

my choice.

he narrates,
fiction—
fantasy.

i write,
my truth—
reality.

untethered—
free.

<u>**day twelve**</u>
**letting go**

last night i heard a song—

that reminded me of you.


i listened—

not a waterfall,

just a trickle, not a flood.


i watched a movie in bed

not one thought of you appeared.

when i realized it,

i was stunned.


i didn't dream of you.


i set my alarm for later—

because sleep is better—

than driving to an empty lot.


the drive to work held no trace of you.

when i parked,

i knew:

im managing to let go.


i write this now—

without sadness,

anger,

or ache.


only calm reflection.


we are like an echo

silently fading—


goodbye.

## day thirteen
**texting**

our method of connection—

my phone on mute,

always checking

to hear from you.


a reflex ingrained

deep in my brain.


when it stopped,

i still couldn't

refrain.


i started writing

my feelings down

pretended—

i was texting you.


after some time,

my head—

started to clear.

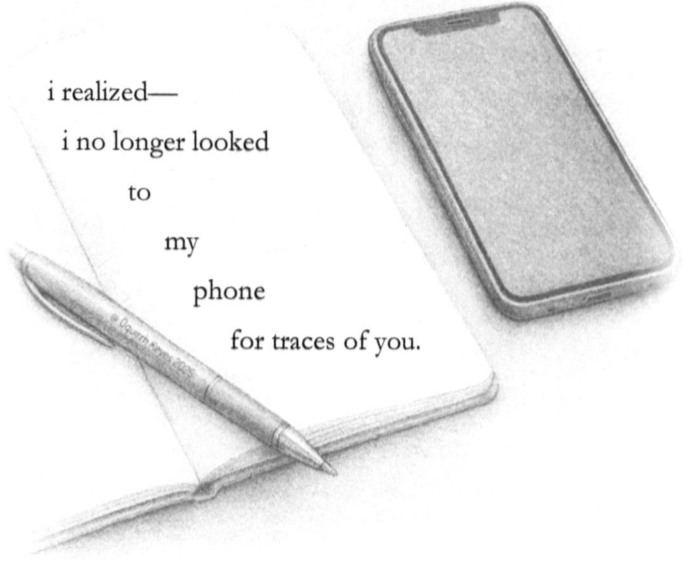

i realized—

i no longer looked

to

my

phone

for traces of you.

<u>**day fourteen**</u>
**vacation**

my first trip without you.
no watchful eye on my location,

no *are you safe?* or *come home soon.*

i don't worry about cell service,
or wifi to send you proof—
no pictures offered as payment,
no intrusion into my family's time.

i put the phone away,
focus on right now,
and breathe into the moment.

my mind unclenches,
finally at rest.

a trip without you—
my first in years.

<u>**day fifteen**</u>
**parallel**

i lived two lives,

one in the open,

one in the shadows.


at first i thought i could be both,

but the fracture deepened,

and i lost myself in the switch.


the walls blurred,

the noise bled through.


neither life was whole.


chaos ensued.


today i choose one life—

my own,

unhidden,

finally whole.

<u>**day sixteen**</u>
**peace**

i'm doing fine.


the smiles come easy,
the tears are few.


i don't ache for you,
in everything i do.


calm drifts over me,
a long breath released—
my mind empties.


**peace.**

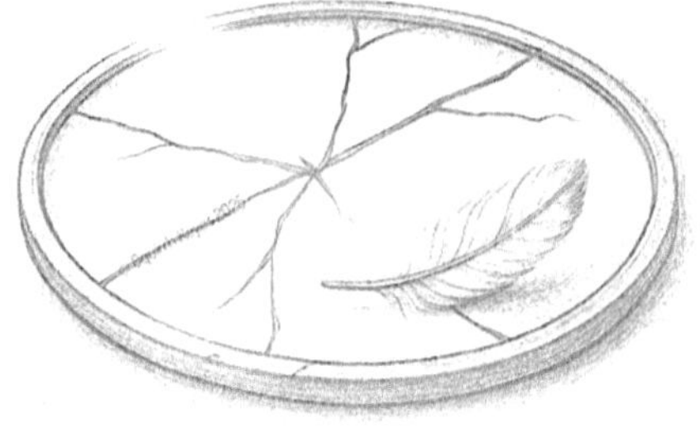

my mind is blank.


no words about you—
or us.


our history is dust.


i feel empathy for her,
i can see now,
you painted her untrue.


you betrayed us both
gaslit us full-time—
a litany of lies
was all we knew.


two women learning,
the truth.


no longer—
circling,
you.

return to sender
@Oquirrh Keyes 2025

<u>**day eighteen**</u>
**you've got mail**

the email came—
vague, reaching.


the tug at my heart
no longer pulled.


it reminded me of our beginning,
when emails were our only tether.


i answered a craigslist ad—
back then, it felt apropos.


here we are,
full circle:
years of texts,
facetimes, calls—
touch and togetherness
reduced to an email.


like the start—
when i waited for a
stranger's reply.

only this time

i don't want to connect.

your email came—

i marked it spam.

**<u>day nineteen</u>**
**gravity**

last night—

you understood,

the door was really shut.


today i returned my cuff—

the final fracture done.


i waited for tears,

for some sharp ache—

nothing happened inside me.


i saw your rear-view mirror—

 bare.


the little heart-rock i gave you

gone—

a silent confirmation

you'd already moved on.


i placed the box

in the bed of your truck—

an easy task to do,

i drove away with

nothing in my chest—

no grief,

no weight.


only silence.


in that silence,

my final adieu.

**<u>day twenty</u>**
**unmissed**

i thought i'd feel more today.


i didn't miss coffee,
i didn't miss you.


i was focused at work—
the first in a month.


i looked out the window toward you
and discovered the sky—
dark, cloudy, a storm arrived.


its rain replaced the tears
i used to shed.


the rain washed away you.

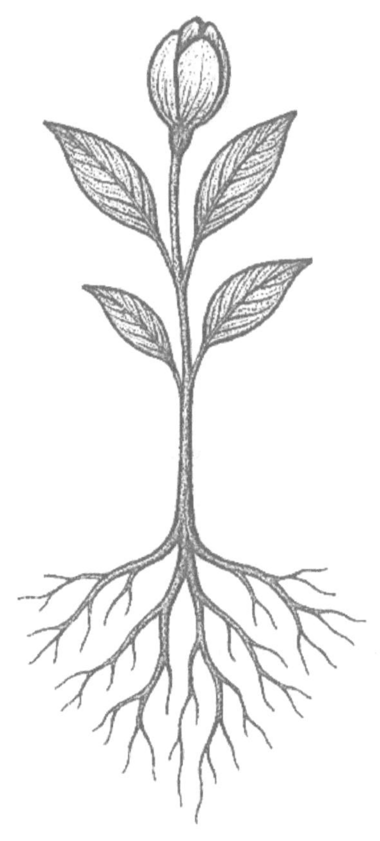

<u>**day twenty-one**</u>
**roots**

i'm enjoying music again.

i can think of you without crying.

i'm not angry anymore.

i slept deep—
the first time in weeks.

my presence at home,
has made me look—
at my husband,
with warmth.

in return—
he is becoming the man
i fell in love with,
many years ago.

your absence made me feel—
like i was going to die.

your silence made me grow cold.

the cloud has lifted,
and i can see—
my roots are strong
just neglected—
attention,
has made them bloom.

we were never meant to be,
and that's not killing me.

## day twenty-two
**no contact**

two steps forward,

one step back.


i broke the silence today,

cracked the shell of no contact,

let the thread unravel again.


what have i done?


it doesn't erase

the steps i've taken,

the truths i've spoken,

the silence i've claimed.


it only reminds me—

how heavy the tether was,

how strong the pull can be.


two steps forward,

one step back—

still, i am moving,

still, i am leaving,

still, i am learning
to walk without you.

72

<u>**day twenty-three**</u>
**deflections**

i asked,

you answered—

semi-truths.

but i already knew.

i held up the proof.

you admitted—

trying to soften the blow.

i thanked you for honesty.

my suspicions confirmed.

ten years—

all lies.

and still,

i'm sad for you.

a. Dqurrh Keyes 2025

## <u>day twenty-four</u>
**i still care**

i don't want you back,
but i still care.

i loved you once—
not lightly, not halfway.

all in, deeply—
i fell—hard.

and though i'm walking away,
i don't wish you ruin.

i hope you find yourself,
i hope you learn peace.

love doesn't vanish,
it just changes shape.

mine has folded inward now,
back into me.

but a trace remains,
quiet as breath—

i don't want you back,
but i still care.

**<u>day twenty-five</u>**
**just me**

even now,

after all these days,

i sit here stunned—

no us,

just me.


i imagine it's a dream,

that tomorrow will bring coffee,

your grin,

your warm embrace.


i imagine us exploring—

taking pics,

laughing,

enjoying the food i made.


these are the moments

that never fade—

a reel of us,

plays on repeat—

even though,

the screen

has gone black

40,4654°N
112.0844°W

<u>**day twenty-six**</u>
**yellow fork canyon**

it rained that day—

lightning,

hail,

mother nature on display.


our first adventure—

yellow fork canyon.


we hiked, had a picnic—

but even then,

i knew.


you were silent,

almost sad,

your mind somewhere else.


the weather stormy

dark—

foreboding,

all the clues were there.

she had left you

or pushed you away—

the story i never knew.


i felt it that day

in all the words—

you didn't say.


my intuition is strong,

i ignored it for you.


later you gave me a bracelet

with coordinates of that canyon.


you said it was for when

i was feeling lost—

a reminder of you.


i wore it

because you wore one too.


now i see—

that feeling of being lost,

the bracelet you gave—

were really for you.

a moment in time

when you might have felt safe.


it's always been about you.

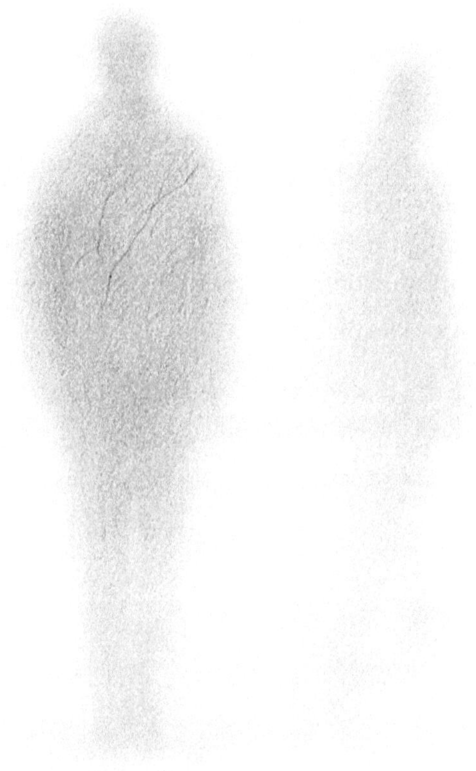

<u>**day twenty-seven**</u>
**what if**

i will forever wonder
what if.


what if love had been whole,
what if truth had been enough,
what if the world we built
wasn't made of shadows and lies.


the ache asks the question,
but the answer never comes.


because the man in my "what-ifs"
doesn't exist,
just you.


what is,
is enough for me—
to let the what ifs go.


so i do…

…what if?

## <u>day twenty-eight</u>
**intense**

this week was intense—
your words, not mine.


i no longer wear our cuff,
given back to you.


it made me panic,
and i contacted you.


we exchanged texts,
conversation ensued.


finally we both
spat out hurtful words—
something we'd never done—
stress had finally won.


a night passed in silence.


the next morning,
we continued—

no hate,

no anger,

just talking about the future—
one where we were strangers.

i grasp this wholly,

not sad—
looking ahead.

you circle the block,
not forward at all.
you cling to failed fantasy—
that is it,
that is all.

i woke up this morning

at peace,

more aware.

my future looks brighter.
i'm ready—
more prepared.

# day twenty-nine
**reflex**

it snowed.


my mountain is white.


i grabbed my phone,
took a pic,
and almost sent it to you.


i giggled
when i remembered—
you're caged,
not me.


i changed the number,
sent it to my husband—
the man who really cares.


his response was simple,
genuine:
*"how pretty,*
*hurry home".*

<u>**day thirty**</u>
**sunday**

i spent the day
with my family—
we ran errands,
had lunch.

a long drive
just to see.

time well spent
enjoying it all—
i was present,
not lost in fantasy.

going home,
i noticed a truck,
tundra,
grey—
like the one you drive.

today,
i didn't look
to see
who's inside.

just let go

# <u>day thirty-one</u>
## counting

i've been counting the days—

silently,

inside.


i think this is no longer

about you.


my healing is forming—


far from complete—


but marking the days
gives you weight.


**i won't count anymore.**


the quiet taught me
how to listen.


what remains now
is memory.

**reflection**

at the end of day thirty-one
i stopped counting.

the ache softened
into memory.

i still think of you,
but the thoughts don't sting—
they simply exist,
pass through—
dissipate.

time hasn't healed everything.

it just made space—
to store memories,
erasing pain—
allowing
new memories
to be made.

the quiet calandre

time not marked on the calendar

CONTRACT
fine
print

**after careful review**

two months ago—
i thought i wanted this,
you telling me—
i was the one,
all along.


after careful review—


of everything
we both said,
it became
evident:
you're broken,
beyond repair.


and though—
you aren't
intentionally cruel,
a healthy love
you'll never achieve.

so please—

don't come

begging.

not for me.

**november**

close to three months—
i don't really think about
you.

you cross my mind—
from time to time.

little things remind me,
but they fade
just as i recall—
the futility
of it all.

you still text,
try to meet.

your history
on repeat.

all i can think—
go home to your wife.

fix your life.

stay away from me.

**waves**

it comes in waves—
nothing concrete,
no single moment
seen.

it happens—
gradually.

you think—
you have it,
and then you falter.

it's a puzzle,
pieces placed—
painfully slow.

it doesn't erase,
or make you feel less—
it just shows up
when you aren't looking.

it says—


"*hey. hello*".


closure—
takes time.


i've finally—
found mine.

**java joes**

i avoided driving by
this shop—
the place you used to stop—
to get our morning
fix.

the place that
knew our order by
heart,
prepared and
waiting—
before you pulled
up.

i'd go on mornings
you were running late—
they knew,
me too.

today i made the stop.

no order
waiting—

it had been so long.

i was asked
if i needed two.

i said,
*just one*—
from now on.

the other—
is
**dead.**

**movement**

i thought it would take a year,
maybe longer,
to move through the loss of you.

a year of silence—
pressing against my chest.

a year of questions—
with no answers.

but it wasn't time
that shifted the weight—
it was honesty.

naming what was real,
accepting what was broken,
writing it down.

until it felt lighter.

the ache is still here,
but it no longer feels endless.

it has softened—

into something,

i can carry.


i thought it would take a year.

it took less.


not because i am strong,

but because i finally stopped

hiding—

from the truth.


i put,

pen to paper—

wrote my truths.


made them poetry—

music on paper.


something new—

about me,

not you.

**note to self**

a year has passed
since silence consumed me.


the ache softened,
the echoes faded,
and i found rhythm—
in learning to breathe again.


i don't know the future—
that excites me!


what's gone was never wasted—
it shaped me.


my heart is open,
my voice steady,
my feet grounded in reality.


everything is going to be okay—
my life awaits me.

the quiet calendar

## epilogue

i survived the silence.

turns out, healing is loud once it starts talking back.

then came the whispers—
the ones i probably shouldn't say out loud.

i've found my voice.

lowercase no longer required.


**Careless Whispers**

Spring 2026

—Oquirrh Keyes

**Oquirrh Keyes** is a surgical technologist and poet whose work explores truth, silence, and the small rituals that carry us through loss.

Her writing reflects the same steadiness and precision found in healing—measured, deliberate, and deeply human.

*the quiet calendar* is her first full-length collection.